This book was first read by:

· ·

MURRAY THE MILKMAN

Other Murray the milkman stories

 MILK CUP

 THE ENCHANTED HOUSE

ISBN 978-0-9556068-3-0
Published in Great Britain in 2015 By Readaware Limited an imprint of Readaware, Vanston Pl, London, SW6 1BS .

Written By Trovers Orr
Illustrated By Rotlinga Hnamte

Additional Artwork provided by Edmund Hosking, Trovers Orr

Please visit our website: www.readaware.com

Murray the Milkman & Co.

Presents

Milk & Cow

By Trovers Orr

One warm morning Murray the Milkman was driving through Tip Top Village, with his niece and nephew, Dionne and Daniel. They were drinking milk through straws.

Murray said to Dionne and Daniel, "Drink up now. You do not want to waste all of that good milk."

Daniel challenged Dionne to a drinking race. "Last one to finish is a smelly rascal ....On your marks, get set, GO!"

They both started sucking milk through their straws. When the empty slurping noise began Dionne shouted, "Finished!"

Seconds later Daniel shouted "Finished!, It's a draw! A tie!"

"Hold your horses Daniel, no need to tell porky pies. Dionne you won and Daniel slurped a close second", Murray said.

Dionne raised her hands as the winner.

"Uncle Murray, I told Daniel that goats make milk as well as cows, but he said they don't. Is that true?" Dionne asked Murray.

"Of course it's true. Milk only comes from cows" Daniel insisted.

Murray explained to the children, "Well, milk can come from both goats and cows, but most people drink cow's milk."

At that moment they walked into the bakers shop.

"I told you!" Dionne said boastfully.

Both started pulling faces at each other.

"Now, now children….. There are lots of different animals that produce milk for their babies. Not just cows and goats. Also there are types of milk that come from plants and fruits such as almond, soy, rice and don't forget coconut milk."

"Uncle Murray how do you get the milk?" Daniel asked.

"Well you have to 'milk' the cow or goat." Murray answered.

"Milk the cow? How do you milk the cow Uncle Murray?" asked Dionne.

"Well you grip the cow's udder and gently pull . Then the milk comes out", Murray replied.

"Uncle, I don't understand", replied Daniel looking confused.

Murray said, "I think we will have to pay good old Farmer Gribbles a visit and he will explain it to you."

Murray drove to the entrance of Woodland Farm.

Farmer Gribbles was feeding the horses.

"Right on time the milkman has arrived." Farmer Gribbles said to himself.

Beep, Beep. Murray pumped his horn to announce their arrival.

Murray, Daniel and Dionne hopped out of the milk van.

"Hey Farmer Gribbles, I have some special friends, I would like you to meet! Dionne and Daniel."

"Well hello there, It's a pleasure to meet you. Welcome to my farm", Farmer Gribbles replied.

"Hello Farmer Gribbles", they both said with cheerful grins.

"Farmer Gribbles, is there any chances you could show the children, how we make that lovely creamy milk?", Murray asked.

"There is plenty of chance for that to happen. You have come to the right place", Farmer Gribbles said, leading them over to the milk production line.

Farmer Gribbles put the teat suction cups on the cow's udder.

"Doesn't that hurt the cows?" Dionne asked curiously.

"Oh no. The teat cups are gentle so the cows do not feel it much. They enjoy it with a spot of music. They produce some lovely milk", Farmer Gribbles answered.

"Mmm tasty", said Murray in his own world imagining, the freshly produced milk.

Murray was not the only one dreaming of tasty milk. Rascal appeared outside the production shed after finishing his daily exercise.

"Meow Hee Hee. That milkman is not around to catch me this time."

"All that exercise has made me thirsty. I need some milk to keep up my strength", Rascal said sneaking up to the milk van.

"Yummy creamy milk for my tummy. I think I will start with just seven bottles!"

Rascal swiped seven bottles from the milk van and hopped off as fast as his little legs would carry him.

"The milk is mine, all mine. Meowhowhowhowhowwww!", Rascal laughed running away.

Murray, Dionne and Daniel left the milk production shed with Farmer Gribbles.

"Thank you for showing us how milk is produced, Farmer Gribbles." Dionne said gratefully.

"Yeah." agreed Daniel. "It was fun seeing how milk is made. Thank you very much Farmer Gribbles, that was cool".

"You're welcome and come back anytime. Don't forget, we can make cheese, yoghurt and cream from cows' and goats' milk too" Farmer Gribbles told them.

"Bye, Farmer Gribbles", the children said as they ran back into the milk van.

"Thank you very much, Gribbles" said Murray, "The cows look a bit tired after all that milking, does that make them want to sleep?"

"Ooo Nah. The cows lie down when it is going to rain" Farmer Gribbles replied.

They did the milkman handshake then Murray got into the milk van and drove off.

Meanwhile back at the farm, Rascal hid behind the trees about to guzzle the milk.

"Now for my well earned tasty milk. Meow!", said Rascal

Rascal put the bottle to his lips and was just about to take a big swig, when he heard the loudest "MOOO", that he had ever heard.

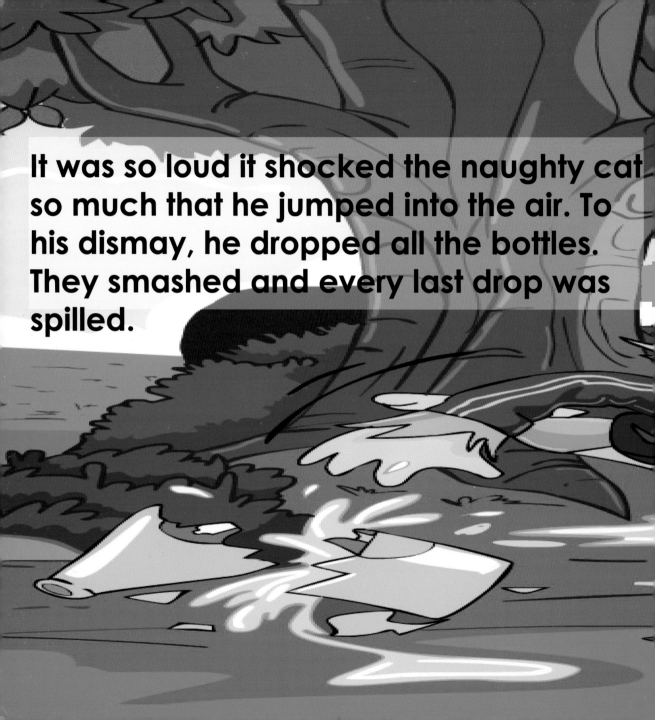

It was so loud it shocked the naughty cat so much that he jumped into the air. To his dismay, he dropped all the bottles. They smashed and every last drop was spilled.